Amy Wild, Animal Talker

The Secret Necklace

Diana Kimpton

Illustrated by
Desideria Gucciardini

The Clamerkin Clan

Hilton

Amy

Einstein

Plato

Isambard

Bun

Willow

To the children of Alderney

First published in the UK in 2009 by Usborne Publishing Ltd., Usborne
House, 83-85 Saffron Hill, London EC1N 8RT, England. www.usborne.com

Text copyright © Diana Kimpton, 2009

Illustration copyright © Usborne Publishing Ltd., 2009

A CIP catalogue record for this book is available from the British Library.

JFMAMJJA OND/09 94248 ISBN 9781409504290

Printed in Great Britain.

CHAPTER ONE

"I want to go home," groaned Amy Wild.

"That's where we *are* going," said Mum
with a smile. She leaned over the rail of the
boat and pointed at the island that lay ahead.
"Clamerkin is our home now."

Amy wiped away a tear with the back of
her hand and glowered at her parents. "I've
told you before. I don't want a new home.
I liked the one we had and I liked my school

and I liked my friends."

"Cheer up, poppet," said Dad, as he put his arm round her shoulders. "The Island of Clamerkin's wonderful. I loved going there on holiday when I was a boy."

"We're sure you'll like it," said Mum. "It's the perfect place for our new beginning."

Amy sighed. It was all right for them. They wanted a simpler life, far away from traffic jams and their old, demanding jobs. But Amy didn't. She had never lived anywhere else but the city. What on earth would she do out here in the middle of nowhere?

As the boat sailed into the harbour, Amy gazed at the buildings perched on the hill behind it. The greyness of their slate roofs was a better match for Amy's gloomy mood than the blue of the late afternoon sky.

"Look at that!" said Dad, pointing at the fields beyond the town. "Wherever you are on Clamerkin, you're always near the country and the sea."

"And look who's come to welcome us," cooed Mum, as a flock of noisy seagulls soared and wheeled overhead. "They're saying they're pleased to see us."

"I bet they're not," said Amy. "They're probably arguing about who gets the next fish." She turned away and concentrated on watching the crew tie the boat up to the harbour wall.

As soon as the gangway was fixed in position, the passengers rushed down it to the shore. Mum and Dad were in the middle of the crowd, carrying their suitcases. Amy stayed as close to them as she could, pulling

her case behind her on its wobbly wheels.
Her stomach was churning with nerves.
Everything here was so different from the city
— even the air smelled different.

Dad ignored the only taxi waiting on the
dock. "We can walk from here. It's not far."
He marched off along the seafront and turned
up a street leading away from the shore.

The wheels on Amy's suitcase rattled
and jolted across the cobbles as she followed her
parents up the hill. The small shops on either
side of the street were closing up for the day.

Most of the shoppers had already gone
home. There were just a few people left,
looking in the shop windows and chatting to
each other. None of them were taking any
notice of Amy. But she had a strange feeling
she was being watched.

For a moment, she thought her imagination was playing tricks. Then she noticed the cats.

There was a slim Siamese outside the post office, a fat black cat down the hill, a scruffy tabby lurking by a drainpipe and a white Persian further up the street. And every single cat was staring straight at Amy. Before she had time to stare back, the wheels on her suitcase finally gave up the struggle. They snapped off and bounced away down the hill. "Bother," groaned

Amy, as the case slammed into the ground.

"Never mind," called a friendly voice. "At least they managed to get you here." Amy looked around, just in time to see the owner of the voice step out from the doorway of the Primrose Tea Room. She was much older than Mum and much rounder. Her long, grey hair was tied back with a bright, red ribbon that matched her red skirt.

Mum nudged Amy in the ribs with her elbow. "Say hello to Great-Aunt Daisy."

The old lady laughed. "Don't call me that. It makes me sound even older than I really am." She smiled at Amy. "I think Granty sounds much better. Don't you, my dear?"

"Yes," agreed Amy in a quiet voice. Meeting her great-aunt for the first time made her feel shy. She wished she already knew her as well as she knew all her other relatives. But Granty never attended family gatherings — the Island was too far away and she hated leaving it.

"That's settled then," said the old lady. She seized hold of Amy's hand and led her towards the door. "Now come inside. Plato and Hilton are dying to meet you."

Amy felt puzzled. She was sure Granty

lived on her own. That's why she needed Mum and Dad to help her run the Primrose Tea Room. So who were Plato and Hilton and why did they have such strange names?

She expected to meet them as soon as she stepped through the front door, but she didn't. The tea room was completely deserted, and there was no sign of any tea. The chairs were piled on the tables, and the only thing on the wooden counter was a large sign saying *CLOSED*.

"It'll be fun getting this place going again," said Dad, as he took down one of the chairs.

"It's got so much potential," agreed Mum, her eyes shining with excitement.

Amy didn't share their enthusiasm. The large room looked dark and gloomy. She wouldn't want to come here for a cup of tea.

And she definitely didn't want to come here to live.

"Come on, Amy," Granty urged. "We mustn't keep Hilton and Plato waiting." She led the way to the back of the room and pushed open a swing door.

Amy hesitated, pointing at the notice on the door that said PRIVATE. "Am I allowed through there?" she asked.

"Of course you are," laughed Granty. "This is your home."

Amy gulped. She hadn't got used to that idea yet. Then she followed the old lady through the door, looking around curiously as she went. She had never been into the private part of a shop before and was surprised to find herself in a very ordinary hallway with a back door at the far end.

A little way ahead, on the right, an open
door gave a glimpse of the kitchen. But
Granty didn't go in there. Instead, she
marched up to the door opposite it — the one
that was firmly closed. "They're both in the
living room," she said, as she flung it open
and pulled Amy inside.

There was a
flurry of paws as
a small bundle
of hair raced
towards them,
yapping loudly. "It's
a dog," squealed Amy in delight.

"*He's* a cairn terrier, actually," said Granty
with great emphasis on the "he". "It's best
not to call animals 'it', my dear. They do get
so offended."

What a curious thing to say, thought Amy. But before she could wonder about it any more, her thoughts were interrupted by a loud squawk. She turned around and saw a brightly coloured parrot watching her from a perch in front of the TV.

"Plato's getting impatient," explained Granty. "He hates Hilton getting all the attention so I'd better introduce you." She pointed at the parrot and said, "Amy — this is Plato." Then to Amy's surprise, Granty pointed at her and added, "Plato — this is Amy."

"Isn't he a lovely bird!" exclaimed Mum, as she walked across the room. Then she pushed her face close to the parrot's and chanted "Who's a pretty boy then?" in a silly voice. Plato was not impressed. He stared at her with what Amy suspected was a look of disgust and shuffled along his perch to a spot as far away from her as possible.

Mum didn't take the hint. She followed him and squeaked, "Pretty Polly, Pretty Polly." Plato gave another loud squawk and shuffled to the other end of his perch. Mum looked disappointed. "It's a shame he can't talk," she sighed.

"He just did," replied Amy. "It's not his fault we're too stupid to understand what he's saying."

"You know that's not what I meant," grumbled Mum, as she went to fetch her suitcase.

"But it is a very interesting comment," said Granty. She turned to the parrot and whispered, "I think Amy may be just the person I've been looking for."

Then she winked at Plato. And, to Amy's astonishment, the parrot winked back.

CHAPTER TWO

Amy didn't have long to wonder about the parrot's strange behaviour, because Mum and Dad whisked her away on a tour of the Primrose. It ended in Amy's new bedroom, which was in the attic, at the top of two flights of stairs.

"We'll leave you to get unpacked," said Mum. "I'm sure you'll feel better when you've settled in."

The room was old-fashioned but appealing. The ceiling sloped, there were yellow roses on the wallpaper and the window looked out over the sea. Amy would have loved it if she was here on holiday. But she wasn't. This wasn't just going to be her room for a week. This was hers for ever, and it was completely different from her room at home — the one she would never see again.

That thought triggered a wave of homesickness, so she went over to the only familiar objects in the whole room — two big boxes standing beside the bed. She knew what was in those. She'd packed them herself, filling them with everything she wanted to send ahead to the Island.

She opened the nearest one and pulled out the bundle of crumpled newspaper that

contained her model animals. She
unwrapped each of them carefully and
arranged them on top of the chest of
drawers. Perhaps they would make this
strange room look more like home.

The last animal she unpacked was a china
cat. The sight of it made her remember the
cats outside in the road. Had they really been
watching her or had she imagined it?

Suddenly something furry brushed
against her leg. She jumped back in surprise
and saw that it was Hilton. She'd been so
absorbed in her task that she hadn't heard
him come in.

The terrier wagged his tail when she
stroked his soft, fluffy head. Amy felt better
with him beside her. Hilton was the best
thing so far about Clamerkin. She had always

wanted a dog, but Dad had said it wasn't fair to have one in the city.

"I'm glad to see you're making friends," said Granty, as she staggered into the room. She dumped the tray she was carrying on the dressing table and sank down onto the bed, puffing and panting. "I'm getting too old for all those stairs. But I thought you'd like some lemonade and cake."

"Thank you," said Amy, as politely as she could. She still felt awkward with her great-aunt, especially after the strange things the old lady had said downstairs.

"Help yourself," said Granty, nodding towards the tray.

Amy didn't need any more encouragement. She had been travelling all day and been too upset to eat anything on the boat. Now the sight of the cake made her realize how hungry she was. It tasted delicious — moist and sweet with a hint of banana. It was also very crumbly, but Amy didn't have to worry about the mess. Hilton happily licked the crumbs off the carpet.

"I do hope you like the room," said Granty. She'd got her breath back by now, and her face looked less red.

"It's lovely," said Amy, without mentioning her homesickness.

"I *am* pleased," replied Granty with a broad smile. "It's such a long time since I was your age. I'm a bit out of touch with what modern girls like."

"I like animals best," said Amy. "And pop music and clothes and stuff like that."

"Hmm," said Granty thoughtfully. "Does jewellery count as stuff?"

"Definitely!"

"Good. Now I wonder what you think of this." Granty put her hands to her throat and lifted something out from underneath her blouse. It was a necklace.

Amy sat down beside her on the bed
and leaned forward for a better
look. She'd never seen
anything like it before. It
was made of metal animal
paws joined together like a
chain. But the metal was dull,
brown and unattractive. It didn't shine at all.

Granty undid the clasp and held the
necklace out to Amy. "Take it, my dear. You
can see it better if you hold it."

Amy didn't like the necklace much. But
she didn't want to offend her great-aunt so
she reached out and took it. As she did so,
Hilton gave an excited bark and jumped up
onto the bed.

Amy looked at him and laughed. He
obviously wanted to see what was going on.

Then she looked back at the necklace she
was holding and stared in amazement.
Something really weird was happening.
The necklace was changing before her eyes.
The dullness was disappearing. The colour
was growing lighter and brighter.

The process only took a few seconds. By
the end of it, the necklace had stopped being

brown and unattractive. Now it was a thing of beauty that gleamed and glittered like pure gold.

Amy turned it over in her hands, trying to work out what had happened. "Is it some sort of trick?"

Granty shook her head and laughed. "You've done that, not me. The necklace stopped working for me as soon as I grew up — it always does for everyone."

A shiver of excitement ran down Amy's spine, mixed with a hint of fear. "What do you mean — it stopped working? What's it supposed to do?"

Granty smiled. "Put it on and see. I promise it won't hurt."

Amy examined the necklace again. It looked completely harmless. If she hadn't seen it change, she would never have suspected there was anything magical about it. She lifted it up slowly, placed it around her neck and fastened the catch.

Nothing happened. There was no clap of thunder, no puff of smoke and her reflection in the dressing-table mirror didn't change at all. Amy felt disappointed. Perhaps the necklace wasn't magic after all. Perhaps Granty had used a conjuring trick to make it change colour.

Then Hilton nudged her hand to attract her attention. "I'm glad you've come," he said. "It's time Clamerkin had a Talker again."

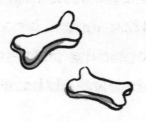

CHAPTER THREE

Amy was too stunned to speak. She stared at the dog, finding it hard to believe what she had just heard. Eventually she found her voice again. "Can you really talk?"

"Of course I can," said Hilton. "So can all animals. We understand each other and we understand humans too. It's only humans who are too stupid to understand us."

"But I'm human and I know what you're

saying." Amy fingered the necklace thoughtfully and turned to Granty. "Is that what this does? Can *you* talk to animals when you're wearing it?"

"Not any more," said Granty. "I'm much too old. The magic only works for children — and not for all of them either. I've been trying to find a new Talker for years, but the necklace refused to work for anyone else until today."

"It's chosen you," squealed Hilton, bounding onto Amy's lap in delight. "Isn't that brilliant?"

He gave her a quick lick on the nose. Then he jumped onto the floor and headed for the door. "I'll go and call the clan together. They'll want to meet you."

Amy's confusion must have shown on her face, because Granty started to laugh. "Don't look so worried."

"What's the clan?" asked Amy.

Granty smiled. "So that's where he's gone. I should have guessed."

Her words reminded Amy that her great-aunt couldn't understand what the dog said. But they didn't answer her question. "So what is the clan?" she asked again.

"You'll find out soon enough," replied Granty. "While you're waiting, you could try out your new skills on Plato. I'm sure he'd love a proper conversation instead of all that 'Pretty Polly' stuff."

"Great," said Amy. "I can show Mum that he really can talk."

Granty suddenly looked serious. "Don't do that!" she warned. "The power of the necklace must always stay secret. It's the only way to make sure it is never misused."

"Mum wouldn't do anything wrong."

"But she would tell other people. You can be sure of that. As soon as you tell one person a secret, it's not a secret any more. And there are too many humans in this world who are willing to use good things for bad ends."

Amy sighed. She was sure her great-aunt was right, but she was disappointed that she couldn't share her excitement about the necklace with anyone else. Then she remembered Plato and realized he was the perfect solution. It was only humans she mustn't tell. She could talk to the animals as much as she liked.

She ran downstairs to the living room. But before she went in, she checked on Mum and Dad. She didn't want them to see her talking to Plato in case they realized she could understand what he was saying. Luckily they were both in the tea room, making plans for the future. They were too busy to notice Amy, so she crept quietly away and went in search of the parrot.

She found him on his perch, watching TV. As she stepped into the room, he put his claw to his beak and whispered, "Shh. It's the last question. If he gets this right, he goes through to the final."

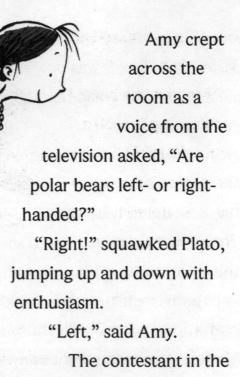

Amy crept across the room as a voice from the television asked, "Are polar bears left- or right-handed?"

"Right!" squawked Plato, jumping up and down with enthusiasm.

"Left," said Amy.

The contestant in the quiz show agreed with Plato. "Right," he announced, but his answer was followed by a dismal hooter.

"That's wrong," said the quizmaster. "All polar bears are left-handed."

"Bother," said Plato. He tipped his head to

one side and stared at Amy. "How did you know that?"

"I read it in a book."

"Reading is such a wonderful skill," sighed the parrot. "I've never quite mastered it myself. That's why I stick to television."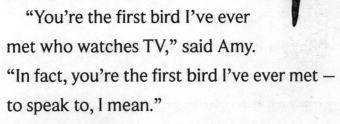

"You're the first bird I've ever met who watches TV," said Amy. "In fact, you're the first bird I've ever met — to speak to, I mean."

"I'm honoured," said Plato, with a little bow. Then he waved a claw towards the necklace. "I'm also delighted to see that around your neck. Have you met the rest of the clan yet?"

Amy shook her head. "I don't even know what it is."

The parrot sat up straight and fluffed out his feathers in a show of importance. Then he gave a little cough and started to explain. "The clan is the group of animals that looks after Clamerkin. We put wrong things right and make sure the Island stays a wonderful place to live."

"We?" said Amy. "So you're part of it."

"So is Hilton," said the parrot. "And, by tradition, so is the Talker — that's you, of course. All the others are cats."

Amy smiled as she remembered the cats who watched her arrive at the Primrose. That didn't seem so strange now. Perhaps they were clan members checking up on her.

She was about to ask if her guess was right, when Hilton burst into the room. "Come into the garden," he panted. "Everyone's ready."

"Off you go, Amy," said Plato. "It's time for you to officially join the clan."

"Aren't you coming?"

Plato shook his head. "I'm more of an advisor really. I don't go to meetings."

"I wish you were coming to this one," said Hilton. "The cats are being difficult." But Plato could not be persuaded to leave his beloved television. He insisted on staying indoors on his perch, leaving Amy and Hilton to go by themselves.

Amy's stomach churned with excitement as she followed the terrier towards the back door. Maybe living on the Island was going to be better than she had expected. She'd only been here a few hours and she already had magical powers and belonged to some secret group she knew nothing about!

Then she remembered Hilton's comment about the cats. What did he mean when he said they were being difficult? Was that going to cause problems for her?

CHAPTER FOUR

Amy had never seen a garden so neglected
as the one that stood behind the Primrose.
The lawn was unmown, the flower beds were
overgrown and the tool shed was rapidly
disappearing under a mound of ivy. Only a
well-trodden path through the long grass
showed that anyone ever went there.

Hilton trotted down it with Amy close
behind. The path led them first to the

washing line and then to what had once been a vegetable patch. A tangled mass of raspberry canes was laden with fruit. Amy couldn't resist picking one as she went past. It tasted delicious — far better than any raspberry from a city supermarket.

But Hilton wasn't interested in eating. He hurried on and disappeared into a dense patch of bushes. That was easy for him — he was small enough to slip under the lowest branches. But Amy was too big to do the same. She had to force her way through the undergrowth until she reached the small clearing where Hilton was waiting.

"This is it," he said. "Welcome to our almost-secret hideout."

"Why *almost-secret*?" asked Amy, as she pulled a bramble out of her hair.

The terrier stared at her as if she was stupid. "If it was completely secret, none of us would ever find it."

Amy scratched her nose thoughtfully. She wasn't entirely sure he was right, but she decided not to argue. "When are the others coming?" she asked.

Hilton looked surprised. "They're already here."

As he spoke, Amy had the same feeling of being watched that she'd first had in the street outside the Primrose. She also remembered what Plato had said about the other members of the clan.

She looked more carefully at the bushes. Now she knew they were there, the cats were much easier to spot. They were the same four as last time — a Siamese, a tabby, a white

Persian and a fat, black cat with white paws.

"That's the good thing about cats," said Hilton. "No one notices them so they find it easy to watch what's going on."

The Siamese jumped down from the branch where she'd been sitting. Then she strode proudly into the clearing. The other three cats followed her and sat in a semicircle on the grass, still staring at Amy.

Hilton bounced from one to the other, sniffing noses in greeting. Amy wondered if she was expected to do the same, but decided against it. So she sat down beside the black cat and waited to see what would happen next.

The cats waited too. Eventually the black one licked his lips. "You don't happen to have a sardine with you?" he asked.

"Sorry. I haven't."

The black cat looked disappointed. But the other three pricked up their ears and stared at her even harder.

"It's true then," said the Siamese. "You really can understand what we say."

"Of course she can," said Hilton. "I already told you that."

"But it was hard to believe," purred the tabby.

Amy put her fingers under the necklace and lifted it slightly away from her throat. "This is what lets me do it. Granty gave it to me."

"So Hilton was right," said the tabby cat. "Her ugly old necklace really is the one the legend talks about." He walked forward, put his front paws on Amy's chest and sniffed at

the string of golden paws. "I wonder how it works. I can't hear an engine."

"That's because it's magic," said the white Persian. "The children were learning about magic beans today. Did you know they grow into giant beanstalks?"

"You shouldn't believe everything you overhear in lessons," said the Siamese. "That's just a story."

"And it's got nothing to do with Amy," added Hilton. "Isn't it about time you introduced yourselves?"

"Stop being so bossy," grumbled the Siamese, as she stood up and whisked her tail from side to side. But she did as she was told. "I'm Willow from the post office. I hear all the news and pass it on to the rest of the clan."

"She means she's a bit of a gossip," explained the tabby. "I'm Isambard, by the way."

"That's an unusual name," said Amy.

"Not for a cat that lives with the local mechanic. I'm named after Isambard Kingdom Brunel, the great engineer."

"I'm called Einstein after the famous scientist," said the white Persian. "The children at school named me when I first went to live there." He waved a paw towards the fat, black cat. "And you've already met our friend from the bakery."

The black cat gazed at Amy with huge green eyes. "A bit of cheese would be almost as good as a sardine," he pleaded.

"Bun!" snapped Willow. "For once in your life, can you please stop thinking of food."

"Sorry," said the baker's cat. He lay down with his head on his paws and sighed. "But my tummy's so empty."

"That's because your tummy's so big," said Einstein.

"Aren't we getting off the subject again?" said Amy. "I thought Hilton had brought me here to join the clan."

Willow arched her back angrily. "He had no right to tell you that," she hissed. "Membership is a matter for the whole clan — not one stupid, little dog."

Hilton gave a low growl in response. "Don't

call me little," he warned. "And you're wrong about Amy. The necklace chose her to be the Talker and the Talker is always a member. It's a tradition."

"It's a legend," argued Willow. "None of us can remember a human ever being part of the clan. It's just a story, like the one about the magic beans."

"Don't you remember Granty — my great-aunt who gave me the necklace? She could talk to animals when she was a child."

"That was years and years before any of us were born," said Einstein. "Dogs and cats don't live as long as humans."

"Parrots do," said Amy. "Surely Plato remembers."

Hilton shook his head. "He's only fifteen. He wasn't even an egg when Granty was young."

"But the necklace really is magic," said Isambard. "There's no doubt about that. So maybe the legend is true too."

Willow wasn't going to give up that easily. "I still say that the necklace doesn't give membership. *We* do. And why should we let her in? We're managing fine without any humans."

"But Amy might help us do even better," suggested Hilton.

"She's got hands," said Bun. "I like hands. They can open sardine tins."

"And use spanners," said Isambard. "None of us can use a spanner."

"None of us need to," said Willow. "The clan has kept the Island safe for as long as we've lived without any interfering human child getting in the way. I don't see why we can't go on doing that."

"I'm not interfering," said Amy, who was tired of them talking about her as if she wasn't there.

"Be quiet," snapped Willow, arching her back again. "This is our decision, not yours." Then she turned to the rest of the clan and added more calmly, "See what I mean. She's already trying to boss us around."

"She's not," said Hilton.

"Why don't we have a vote?" suggested Einstein. "The children at school often vote if they can't agree."

"An excellent idea," said Willow. She
narrowed her eyes into slits and glared at the
other three cats. "Put up your paw if you think
I'm right about not having Amy in the clan."

Einstein and Bun cringed away
from Willow's steely gaze.
Then they both obediently
raised one
front foot.

Only Isambard hesitated.
He stared thoughtfully at
Amy and then at Willow.

"It's a pity
about the spanners,"
he muttered as he slowly
lifted a rather grubby
paw into the air.

Willow looked triumphant. "That's settled then," she purred at Amy. "Talker or not, there's no room for you here." Then she walked away with her tail straight up in the air and started to sharpen her claws on a nearby tree.

Amy was furious. The cats had rejected her without giving her a chance to prove her usefulness. It was so unfair — just like the way Mum and Dad had dragged her to Clamerkin against her will.

That last thought made her explode with rage. "I don't care!" she yelled as she jumped to her feet. "I never wanted to come to your stupid island in the first place, and I certainly don't want to be in your stupid clan!"

CHAPTER FIVE

Amy didn't wait to see the cats' reactions.
She turned and ran, trying to leave her
disappointment far behind. She struggled
through the bushes to the vegetable patch.
Then she raced up the garden towards the
Primrose, with tears stinging her eyes.

Hilton caught up with her as she flung the
back door open. "Come back," he begged.
"I'm sure we can work this out."

"No, you can't. You heard what I said."
She ran inside and wiped her eyes with her
sleeve before she fled into the Primrose's
old-fashioned kitchen.

Mum was already there, helping Granty
cook supper. "Who were you talking to
outside?" she asked.

Amy hesitated. Despite her anger at the
cats, she still didn't want to give away the
secret of the necklace. "Granty's dog," she
replied, picking her words carefully. Surely it
was safe to say that, as long as she didn't
mention that he talked back.

Over by the sink, her great-aunt nodded
approvingly. Amy had obviously made the
right decision.

Mum smiled and started laying four places
on the large, wooden table. "I'm glad you've

got Hilton for company. You'll like the Island much more when you've made some friends."

"If I ever do," muttered Amy so quietly that only she could hear. Maybe everyone else on the Island would be just like the cats. Maybe everyone else would reject her too.

At least Plato seemed to like her. He greeted her warmly when she went into the living room. Then he looked at her miserable face and asked, "Was Hilton right about the cats being difficult?"

Amy glanced over her shoulder to check no one had followed her out of the kitchen. "They won't let me join the clan," she replied, when she was sure that only the parrot could hear her. "They don't care about the necklace or the legend or anything. They say they can manage perfectly well without any human help."

"That's cats for you," said Plato. "They're too independent for their own good."

"They don't like me," moaned Amy.

"They don't know you," said Plato. "This isn't personal. Cats just don't like being told what to do — by dogs or by humans or even by legends."

Amy was still wondering if he was right when Mum called her for supper. It was lasagne — her favourite — but she was too upset to want to eat much. After a few mouthfuls, she pushed her plate away.

"Oh dear," sighed Dad. "Are you still unhappy about coming to the Island?"

"You certainly look miserable," said Granty, with a concerned expression on her face. "Didn't you enjoy your walk with Hilton?"

Amy shook her head. "We met some cats, but they weren't very nice." That was as much as she dared say about the clan meeting while Mum and Dad were listening.

Granty smiled sympathetically. "That's a shame."

Before the old lady could say any more, Mum changed the subject. "What's that?" she asked, pointing at Amy's neck.

"It's a necklace," replied Amy, wishing she'd tucked it inside her T-shirt so it couldn't be seen. "Granty gave it to me."

"I thought it might cheer her up," explained her great-aunt.

"That was kind of you," said Dad. He glanced at her uneaten meal and added, "Pity it hasn't worked."

"Maybe you're just overtired," Mum suggested. "It's been a very long day."

That was just the excuse Amy needed to get away from the table. "You're right," she said, as she pushed her chair back. "I think I'll go to bed early."

As soon as Amy reached her new bedroom,

the events of the day overwhelmed her and she burst into tears. She felt totally alone as she sat on the window seat, hugging her knees and crying. She missed her old home. She missed her friends. But she most definitely did not miss those cats.

Eventually her sobs died away, leaving her empty and exhausted. Now it really was time for bed. She wiped her eyes, blew her nose and changed into her pyjamas. At least they were the same ones as usual. They made her feel a little less homesick.

As she pulled on the top, her fingers touched the necklace. Should she take it off to sleep or leave it where it was? She could see it in the mirror — a gleaming, glittering line around her throat, full of magic and mystery. It still looked as exciting as when

she had first put it on and discovered she
could talk to animals. But that was before the
cats were so horrid to her. Was it really such
a good thing to have?

Despite her doubts, she decided
to keep it on. Still wearing it, she jumped into
bed and dived under the quilt. She wriggled
about, struggling to get comfortable on the

unfamiliar mattress and pillow. Then she lay still and yawned. Mum was right — she was tired.

She was just drifting off to sleep when a high-pitched voice shouted, "Have you seen my cheese?"

Amy's eyes snapped open.

"It's where you left it," yelled a second voice from somewhere behind the skirting board.

"No, it's not. I bet you ate it."

"I didn't."

"Did."

"Didn't."

"Did."

"Didn't."

"Be quiet," yelled Amy. "I'm trying to get to sleep."

The hidden mice went quiet for a moment. Then they started again.

"It's your fault. You were shouting."

"Wasn't."

"Was."

Amy couldn't bear to listen to another word. She snatched the necklace from around her neck and threw it angrily across the room. She didn't bother to see where it landed. She'd had enough of it for one day and didn't care if she never saw it again.

CHAPTER SIX

Early the next morning, Amy woke up to the sound of Hilton barking. He was outside in the corridor, scratching and whining to come in. Amy couldn't understand what he was saying, but she could tell he was anxious about something.

The polished, wooden floor felt cold under her bare feet as she ran across the room. As soon as she opened the door, the terrier rushed inside, barking wildly. He jumped up at Amy and knocked her off-balance, so she sat down suddenly on the end of the bed.

Hilton threw himself onto her lap, still barking. Then he stared at her bare neck, put his head back and gave a long, low howl. It was the most miserable sound Amy had ever heard. And she knew immediately what was wrong. Hilton had spotted that she wasn't wearing the necklace. Without that, she would never understand what he wanted.

"I threw it over here somewhere," she said, as she started searching the area where it might have landed. Hilton joined in, sniffing under the chair and scrabbling through the contents of the waste-paper bin.

But there was no sign of the necklace.

It had completely vanished. Amy was about to give up in despair when she had an idea. She jumped back into bed and threw her comb across the room, just as she had thrown the necklace the night before.

It landed on her chest of drawers, slid across the top and fell down the back. "That's the answer," yelled Amy. "It's the one place we haven't looked."

The chest was made of solid wood and very heavy. It took all Amy's strength to heave it a few centimetres away

from the wall. Then she lay down and reached into the dark space behind it.

She quickly found the comb and pulled it out. Then she pushed her hand back in and searched again. At first, she felt nothing but dust. But she wasn't ready to give up yet. So she stretched out as far as she could, reaching further and further until finally her probing fingers touched metal.

"Got it," she yelled, as she caught hold of the necklace and pulled it out.

The chain of animal paws had turned brown and dull again. But it was already changing now it was back in contact with her. Amy stared in fascination, as the paws started to glitter and gleam just as they had when she had held it for the first time.

Hilton's impatient bark reminded her why she had been looking for the necklace in the first place. As quickly as she could, she placed it round her neck and fastened the catch.

"Thank goodness for that," said Hilton. "Now come with me — there's an emergency. The clan's been called out."

"But I'm not in it. You heard Willow. They don't need me."

"Yes, they do. They're just too stupid to realize it. And it doesn't matter anyway.

You're not coming as a clan member. You're coming as my friend."

Amy couldn't argue with that. She threw on her clothes as quickly as she could. Then she bounded down the stairs after Hilton.

She popped into the kitchen, slipped a couple of items into her pockets for later and wrote a note to Mum saying she'd gone for a walk with Hilton. Then she ran back into the hall, opened the back door and stepped out into the early morning sunshine.

This time Hilton didn't take her down the garden. Instead, he led her along a side path into the street. Then they both raced down the hill towards the harbour.

"It's Oscar," explained the terrier as they ran. "He's gone missing."

"Who's he?" asked Amy.

"One of Tabitha's kittens — the ginger one." Hilton skidded to a halt outside a shop window full of flowers. The name above it said *Bob and Betty's Blooms*. So did the green lettering on the van parked outside.

Amy followed the terrier into a narrow alley that separated the flower shop from the baker's next door. She spotted the cats straight away. There were five of them this time. The four clan members were gathered around a grey cat who looked utterly miserable. Amy guessed she was Tabitha.

Willow's eyes opened wide in alarm when she saw the new arrivals. Her tail shot straight up in the air and the hairs on it stuck out like bristles on a bottlebrush. "What's she doing here?" she demanded.

"I brought her," said Hilton. "The more eyes we've got searching, the sooner we'll find Oscar."

"My poor Oscar," wailed Tabitha. "It's all my fault."

"No it's not," said Willow, in a much

kinder voice than Amy had heard her use before. "You didn't tell him to run away."

"But I didn't check he was safe," wailed Tabitha, who was not going to be comforted that easily. "I'd just finished counting them all and settling them for bed when I 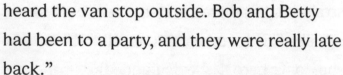 heard the van stop outside. Bob and Betty had been to a party, and they were really late back."

"What's that got to do with Oscar?" asked Einstein.

"They opened the front door," said Tabitha. "That's when Oscar must have slipped out, and I'm such a bad mother that I didn't notice." She started to wail again.

"Now, now," said Isambard. "There's no use crying over spilled milk."

Bun's ears pricked up. "Is there some milk? I could really do with a drop right now."

The others ignored him. "Where do you think he might have gone?" asked Isambard.

"He's very curious," said Willow. "Whenever I visit, he's always got his nose into something."

"And he's fascinated by the sea," added Tabitha. "He loves watching it from the window, and he's always asking questions about it."

"Maybe that's where he's gone," suggested Hilton. "I bet he spotted his chance and ran off to explore the beach."

"He picked the right time to do it," said Einstein. "It was a really low tide last night so there would have been masses of rocks to explore."

Willow's tail did its bottlebrush act again, but this time it wasn't Amy causing the alarm. "The tide's coming back in now," cried the Siamese cat. "Suppose he's got stuck? Suppose he's trapped down there and can't get away?"

"He'll drown!" wailed Tabitha.

"Not if we get there first," said Isambard.

The whole clan raced off down the hill towards the shore. Tabitha stayed behind to care for her remaining kittens. But Amy ran after the clan. She didn't care if the cats were horrid to her now. All that mattered was finding Oscar before it was too late.

CHAPTER SEVEN

The seafront was almost deserted. The
few people who were about were too
preoccupied with their morning chores
to take any notice of Amy and the clan.
Amy was preoccupied too — she was only
interested in finding the lost kitten.

The cats leaped onto the sea wall, slipped
under the railings and jumped down on the
other side. Amy and Hilton raced down the

stone steps instead
and caught up with
the cats on
the beach.

"About time
too," muttered
Willow.

Isambard seemed
more welcoming.
"Spread out, everyone.
We'll start here and work
our way towards the sea.
But we must hurry — the tide's
already coming in."

"Wouldn't it be better to start as close to
the sea as we can get?" Amy suggested.
"Otherwise some of the beach will be
covered with water before we can search it."

The Siamese cat glared at her. "Interfering again!" she snapped.

"But it's a good idea," said Einstein.

"Definitely," Isambard agreed. "Forget what I said before. We'll start the search at the water's edge."

Amy immediately set off towards the line of gently breaking waves. The beach was much wetter near the sea. Her feet squelched on the sodden sand and slithered on the damp, slippery rocks.

Isambard was right — the tide was coming in. Each wave swished further up the beach than the one before. Soon the rocks she was standing on would disappear completely under the rising water. They must find Oscar before it was too late.

She bent down and peered into every

nook and cranny, searching for the missing kitten. A little way to her right, Hilton was looking too — scrabbling among the rocks with his head down so he could use his nose as well as his eyes. The cats were more agile than him, leaping nimbly from rock to rock as they searched. Even Bun was surprisingly athletic for an animal with such a fat stomach.

Suddenly a flock of seagulls swooped low overhead. "What are you doing? What are you doing?" they chorused.

"Looking for a lost kitten," Amy shouted back.

"A ginger one," added Hilton.

"We'll help. We'll help," chorused the seagulls. They flew off across the beach, swooping down to inspect the rocks.

Occasionally one of them landed to investigate a possible hiding place, before taking off again calling, "No luck, no luck."

"This is brilliant," said Hilton. "They can search must faster than us."

"If they find him, I'll never chase another bird," said Bun.

"You never chase birds anyway," said Einstein.

At that moment, the seagulls soared back and wheeled in circles over Amy and the clan. "No kitten, no kitten," they chorused. "He's somewhere else. He's somewhere else."

Willow yowled with frustration. "We've been looking in the wrong place."

"At least, we know he's not going to drown," said Einstein, as they all set off towards the steps.

"That doesn't mean he's safe," said Willow. "We still don't know where he is."

"And we've got our feet wet for nothing," Bun moaned.

Amy had forgotten how much cats dislike water. They were jumping from rock to rock, trying to keep out of it as much as they could. When that wasn't possible, they tiptoed across the wet sand as fast as possible. The looks of disgust on their faces made it obvious how they felt.

"We should have realized Oscar wouldn't like the beach," said Isambard, when they were safely back on the seafront. "It's much too damp."

"So what sort of places *do* cats like?" asked Amy.

Willow stared at her as if she was stupid.

"Dry ones, of course."

"I like sleeping in the baker's shop window," said Bun. "It's lovely and warm when the sun shines through the glass."

"I like curling up beside the school boiler," said Einstein. "That's deliciously warm too."

"What about you, Willow?" asked Amy. "Where's your favourite spot in the post office?"

"On the shelf above the radiator, if you must know," replied the Siamese. "But we're wasting time. This isn't helping us find Oscar."

"It might," said Amy. "He slipped outside when Bob and Betty came home. Then they shut the door behind them, leaving him stuck outside in the cold. All of you like sleeping somewhere warm, so I'm sure Oscar does too. All we've got to do is find the warm spot where he's gone to sleep."

Hilton jumped up and down with excitement. "Brilliant," he yelped, showing all his teeth in a big doggy grin. "So what's the warmest spot near Tabitha's?"

"There's a nice sunny spot beside the gooseberry bush," suggested Bun.

Isambard shook his head. "That won't be warm at night."

"The wood store's quite comfy," suggested Willow.

"But it's draughty," said Einstein. "It's not really warm."

There was a long pause while they all thought hard. Amy tried to picture the events of last night in her head. She imagined the van stopping outside the flower shop, Bob and Betty opening the front door and the adventurous ginger kitten running out into the dark.

Then she put herself in Oscar's place, trying to see what he had seen. It was late. There was no one else around. There was only one thing in the deserted street that might have caught the kitten's attention.

"What about the van?" she asked. "That would be warm, wouldn't it?"

"Naturally," said Isambard. "Tabitha's humans had only just driven home."

"But we'd have seen him if he'd been on top," said Willow.

"And he definitely wasn't underneath," added Einstein. "I know — I checked."

"He couldn't have got inside either," said Hilton. "The doors and windows were shut."

Amy's shoulders slumped with disappointment. Perhaps the van wasn't the answer after all. Then she had an idea. "What about the place where the engine is? Could Oscar be in there?"

"Clever thinking," shrieked Isambard as he bounded to his feet. "That must be where he is. A cat can easily wriggle into the space under the bonnet, and it's a wonderfully warm spot when the engine's just been running." He stared wistfully into space and added, "I love engines. They're so noisy and powerful."

"And dangerous!" cried Willow in alarm. "We've got to get him out of there before Bob starts it up." She raced off up the hill towards the flower shop with the others close behind.

They were only halfway up
when they saw Bob step out of the
front door and walk towards the van.

"Hurry, hurry," cried Willow.

"We've got to stop him," barked Hilton.

Amy didn't say anything. She was too out
of breath and too far behind. She couldn't
run as fast as the others. But she didn't give
up. She had to help save Oscar before it was
too late.

CHAPTER EIGHT

"Don't start the van!" barked Hilton, as he rushed up to Bob.

The owner of the flower shop glanced at him, obviously wondering what all the fuss was about. But he couldn't understand what the terrier was saying, so he just ignored him. He stepped towards the van and unlocked the door.

"Don't start the van!" shrieked Einstein,

launching himself at Bob like a white, furry torpedo. He landed on the man's arm, slipped sideways and dug in his claws to save himself.

"Let go," shouted Bob, as he shook off the Persian cat that was hanging from his sleeve.

"Don't start the van!" cried Bun and Isambard together. The tabby cat attached himself to Bob's other arm while Bun rushed in front of the flower seller's feet to block his path.

"Stop it, all of you," yelled Bob. "Have you lot gone bananas?"

The clan didn't stop. They went on barking and yowling the warning that the human couldn't understand. But he was bigger than all of them. They couldn't stop him opening the van door.

Willow jumped bravely onto the driver's seat. She arched her back and made her tail do its bottlebrush act again. "Don't start the van!" she hissed. But Bob couldn't understand *her* either.

"That's enough," he yelled angrily. He hauled the Siamese cat out of the van and dumped her on the pavement. As Amy pounded up to the van, he sat down on the seat and reached out to put the keys in the ignition.

Amy pushed her hand over the keyhole, just in time to stop him. "Don't start the van," she begged.

Bob looked puzzled. "Why ever not?"

"Because I think there's a kitten asleep on your engine."

Bob's anger was immediately replaced by concern. He jumped out of the van, ran to the front and lifted the bonnet. Amy and the clan gathered round him, jostling to get a good view inside.

Oscar was curled up on top of the engine — a splash of ginger against the black, oily metal. The noise and commotion had woken him up. He yawned and peered at his rescuers with big, blue eyes. "I want my mum," he mewed.

"Just look at that," said Bob. "It's a good thing you stopped me, little girl."

"My name's Amy," said Amy, who shared Hilton's dislike of being called little. "I've just come to live at the Primrose."

"It's a jolly good thing you have," said Bob, as he lifted the ginger kitten to safety. "Otherwise this little fellow would have had a nasty accident."

Amy and the clan followed him indoors. They stayed just long enough to see Oscar happily reunited with Tabitha. Then they slipped away before Bob started asking awkward questions. Amy didn't want to explain how she knew the kitten was there.

"That's a job well done," said Hilton, when they reached the almost-secret hiding place.

"Definitely," said Isambard.

"All that running around has made me hungry," said Bun.

"That's not surprising," said Einstein. "Even lying down makes *you* hungry."

Bun looked appealingly at Amy. "I don't suppose you happen to have a sardine with you, by any chance."

Amy laughed. "It's funny you should ask," she replied as she pulled a tin of sardines out of one pocket and a can-opener out of the other. It seemed ages ago that she had picked them up on her way through the kitchen.

Bun looked over at Willow. "You see — humans *can* be useful."

"I know," said the Siamese cat. She hung her head low in shame. "I'm sorry I was so horrid yesterday, Amy. We would never have saved Oscar without you."

"That's okay," said Amy. "I'm glad I was able to help."

Willow perked up. "I think the legend may be right after all. Who thinks we should follow tradition and let the Talker join us?"

Amy held her breath as she waited for their response. She didn't have to wait long. Without any hesitation, Hilton, Isambard, Einstein and Bun all raised one front paw in the air.

Then Willow did the same. "We're all agreed," she purred. "Welcome to the clan, Amy Wild. You're now a full member."

Amy whooped with delight and hugged Hilton. Then the four cats rushed over, determined not to be left out of the fuss.

"I'm going to like having you here," said Bun as he tucked into the sardines.

"And I'm going to like being here," said Amy. For the first time since she got off the boat, she really felt at home. Life on Clamerkin was going to be much more fun than living in the city.

The End

Amy Wild, Animal Talker

Collect all of Amy's fun and fur-filled adventures!

The Musical Mouse

There's a singing mouse at Amy's school! Can Amy
find it a new home before the headmaster catches it?

ISBN 9781409504306

The Mystery Cat

Amy finds a cat who's lost his memory and promises
to track down his owners. But she's in for a surprise!

ISBN 9781409504313 (Coming in 2010)

The Furry Detectives

Things have been going missing on the Island and
Amy suspects there's an animal thief at work...

ISBN 9781409504320 (Coming in 2010)

All priced at £4.99